For Will and Nate   —HZ

For Anna   —RD

Text copyright © 2002 by Harriet Ziefert
Illustrations copyright © 2002 by Rebecca Doughty
G. P. PUTNAM'S SONS,
a division of Penguin Putnam Books for Young Readers, 345 Hudson Street, New York, NY 10014.
G. P. Putnam's Sons, Reg. U.S. Pat. & Tm. Off. Published simultaneously in Canada.
Printed in China for Harriet Ziefert, Inc.
Jacket designed by Carolyn T. Fucile.
Text set in Gill Sans. The art was done in Flashe paint and ink on bristol board.
Library of Congress Cataloging-in-Publication Data
Ziefert, Harriet. Toes have wiggles kids have giggles / Harriet Ziefert;
illustrated by Rebecca Doughty. p. cm.
Summary: Rhyming text presents the characteristics of things
which are frequently experienced or observed in the lives of children.
[1. Day—Fiction. 2. Stories in rhyme.] I. Doughty, Rebecca, ill. II. Title.
PZ8.3.Z47 To 2002 [E]—dc21 2001048248
ISBN 0-399-23617-1
10 9 8 7 6 5 4 3 2 1
First Impression

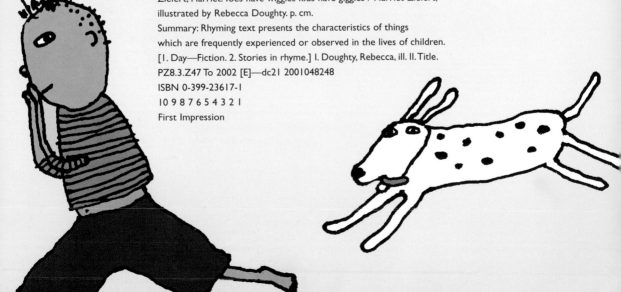

Toes Have Wiggles Kids Have Giggles

by Harriet Ziefert

drawings by Rebecca Doughty

G. P. Putnam's Sons   New York

Summers have bicycles.

Winters have icicles.

polkas have dots.

Paints
have
blots.

Naps
have
cots.

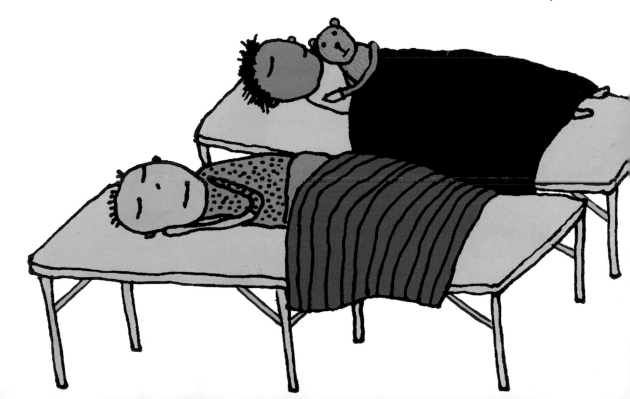

Donuts
have
custard.

Hot dogs
have
mustard.

Doors
have
bells.

Wishes
have
wells.

Flowers have smells.

Cats have rubs.

Baths have
tubs.

Brushes have
scrubs.

Days have

Mosquitos
have
bites.

nights.

pillows have fights.

Lollies have

Ponies have

Kicks.

licks.

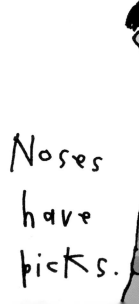

Noses
have
picks.

Grown-ups have careers.

Good-byes have tears...

Kids have ears.

Faucets
have
drips.

Chips
have
dips.

Kisses have lips.

Faces have

Dogs
have
growls.

scowls.

Batters
have
fouls.

Monsters
have
hairy.

Squirrels have stash.

potatoes
have
mash.

pools
have
a splash.

Cowboys have horses.

Magnets
have
forces.

Libraries have lends...

Letters have sends.

Books
have
ends.

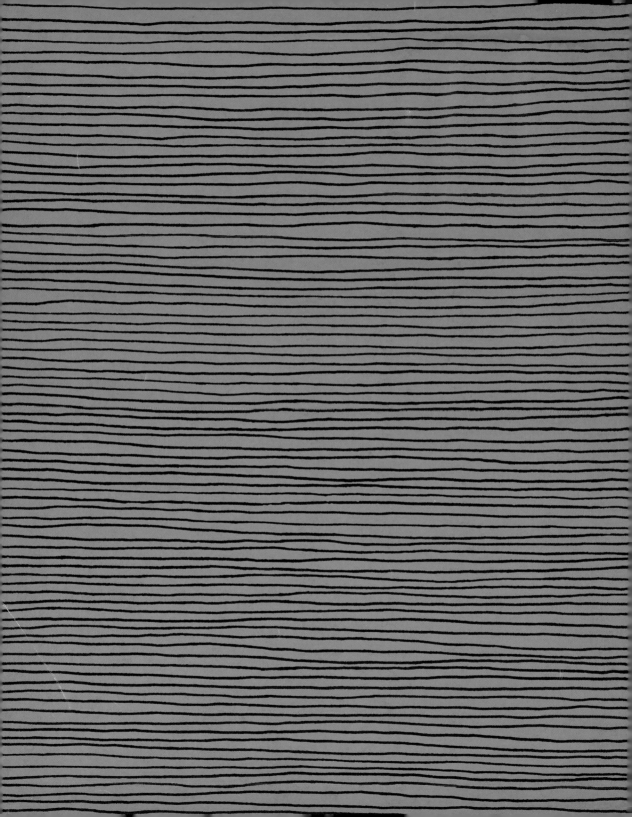